A NOTE TO P...

D0343102

Congratulations on choosing the best in educational materials for your child. By selecting top-quality McGraw-Hill products, you can be assured that the concepts used in our books will reinforce and enhance the skills that are being taught in classrooms nationwide.

And what better way to get young readers excited than with Mercer Mayer's Little Critter, a character loved by children everywhere? Our First Readers offer simple and engaging stories about Little Critter that children can read on their own. Each level incorporates reading skills, colorful illustrations, and challenging activities.

Level 1 – The stories are simple and use repetitive language. Illustrations are highly supportive.
Level 2 - The stories begin to grow in complexity. Language is still repetitive, but it is mixed with more challenging vocabulary.
Level 3 - The stories are more complex. Sentences are longer and more varied.

To help your child make the most of this book, look at the first few pictures in the story and discuss what is happening. Ask your child to predict where the story is going. Then, once your child has read the story, have him or her review the word list and do the activities. This will reinforce vocabulary words from the story and build reading comprehension.

You are your child's first and most influential teacher. No one knows your child the way you do. Tailor your time together to reinforce a newly acquired skill or to overcome a temporary stumbling block. Praise your child's progress and ideas, take delight in his or her imagination, and most of all, enjoy your time together!

Library of Congress Cataloging-in-Publication Data

Mayer, Mercer, 1943-
    No one can play / by Mercer Mayer.
        p. cm. – (First readers, skills and practice)
    Summary: When no one will play with Little Critter one day, he uses his imagination to find new friends, including a mouse, a frog, and a spider. Includes activities.
    ISBN 1-57768-804-X
        [1. Play—Fiction. 2. Friendship—Fiction.] I. Series.

PZ7.M462 Np 2001
[E]—dc21   2001026661

McGraw-Hill
Children's Publishing

A Division of The **McGraw·Hill** Companies

Send all inquiries to:
McGraw-Hill Children's Publishing
8787 Orion Place
Columbus, OH 43240-4027

Printed in the United States of America.

1-57768-804-X

1 2 3 4 5 6 7 8 9 10 PHXBK 06 05 04 03 02 01

 A Big Tuna Trading Company, LLC/J. R. Sansevere Book

FIRST READERS

Level 1   Grades Pre-K - K

NO ONE CAN PLAY

by Mercer Mayer

 McGraw-Hill
Children's Publishing

4

No one can play today.
What can I do?

6

I can run through the house
with my mouse.

8

I can leap over a log
with my frog.

I can hop in the grass
with my grasshopper.

I can crawl in the leaves with my spider.

I can climb up a tree
with my kitty.

15

I can rest in the shade
with my dog, Blue!

Word Lists

Read each word in the lists below. Then, find each word in the story. Now, make up a new sentence using the word. Say your sentence out loud.

Words I Know	Challenge Words
house	today
mouse	through
log	grasshopper
frog	leaves
grass	spider
tree	shade
kitty	
dog	

Match the Beginning Sound

Name the picture. Think about which two letters make the beginning sound of the picture. Then, match the picture with those letters. The first one has been done for you.

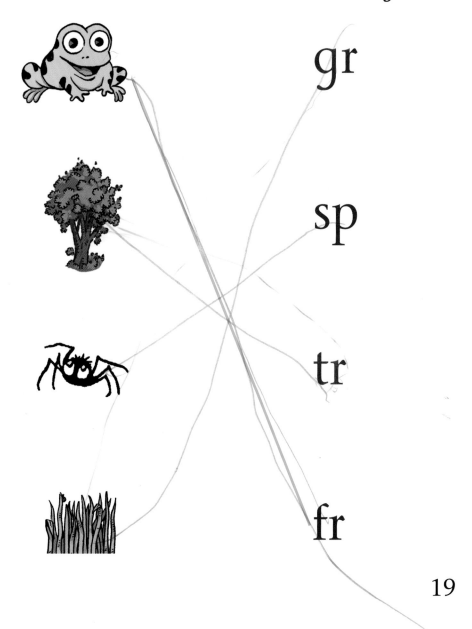

gr

sp

tr

fr

What Happened?

Draw the answers to the questions in the boxes below. If you need help, use the page numbers to find the answer in the story.

Who played with Little Critter by the log? (page 6)

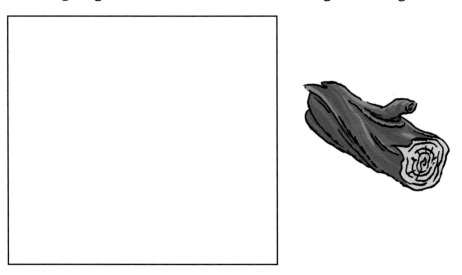

Who played with Little Critter in the leaves? (page 10)

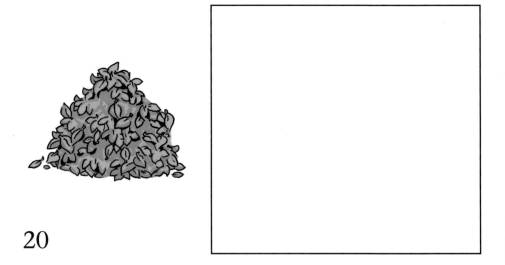

Who played with Little Critter in the house?(page 4)

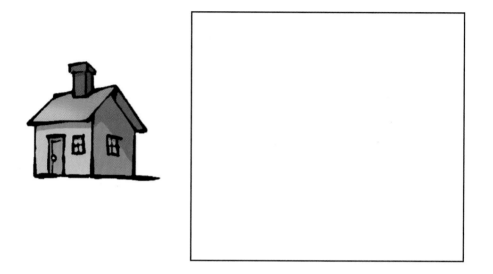

Who played with Little Critter in the tree?(page 12)

The Word I

Did you know that I is both a letter and a word? Use the word I when you are talking about yourself.

Hi! I am Little Critter. I like to play with my pets.

Read the story again. How many times did you see the word I?_____

Trace the word I below. Then, try it on your own. Circle your two best I's.

I I I I